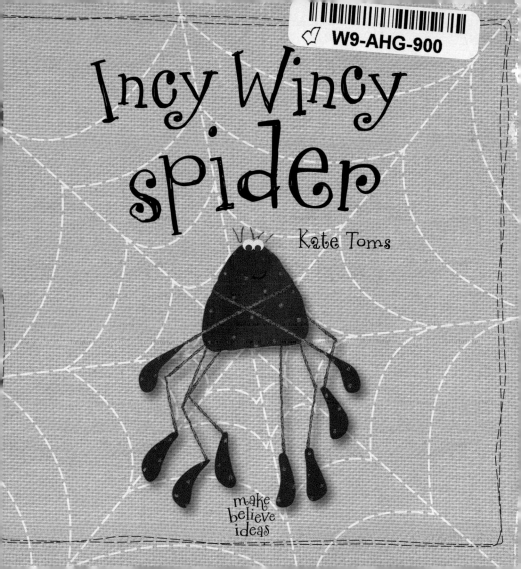

Incy Wincy spider

Kate Toms

make
believe
ideas

Incy Wincy Spider

went UP the water spout.

DOWN came the rain,

and washed the spider OUT.

Out came the SUN

and dried up all the rain,

so Incy Wincy Spider

climbed up the spout again.

Here we go again!

But why does INCY climb the spout?

(In case you are in any doubt.)

Because he's SPUN his web up high,

so he can see the world go by...

(It's easy **dropping** to the floor,

but climbing **UP** is quite a chore.)

Incy Wincy Spider
doesn't like the rain,
he's got his swimming goggles on,
(he won't get
caught again).

But ... just as he starts climbing
up the water spout,
another shower of rain falls down
and
washes
Incy
out!

Uh-oh!

Now **INCY'S** trying once again,

umbrella **at the ready,**

the **rain** won't beat him **this** time

if he takes it

nice and **steady.**

There **has** to be

another way

to get home on a

rainy day!

Looking **round**, what's **Incy** seen?
A **round** and **bouncy** trampoline!

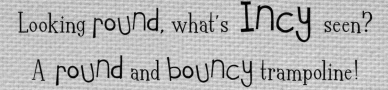

Wheeeee!

He's found a way to get home **fast** ...

Over the hedge,

over the wall,

a stripy tent

breaks his fall.

Looking puzzled,

Incy thinks.

He rubs his hairy head and blinks.

The washing's out
the weather's fine,

Incy wobbles on the line,

when suddenly a breezy breeze blows Incy to some nearby trees.

Through the leaves,
Incy spies

several pairs of

beady eyes.

"But **worse** than that,"
Incy squeaks,

Incy's running, quite puffed out,

but in the distance,

sees the

spout.

It's the best idea
he's had all day.

He'll climb the spout another way.

The rain comes down

nside the spout,

so he'll climb UP

not iN, but out!

Back in his **web**,

he's **happy** now.

(It's easy when you've worked out how …)

The lesson **learned?**

Try, try again …

and don't be put off by the rain!

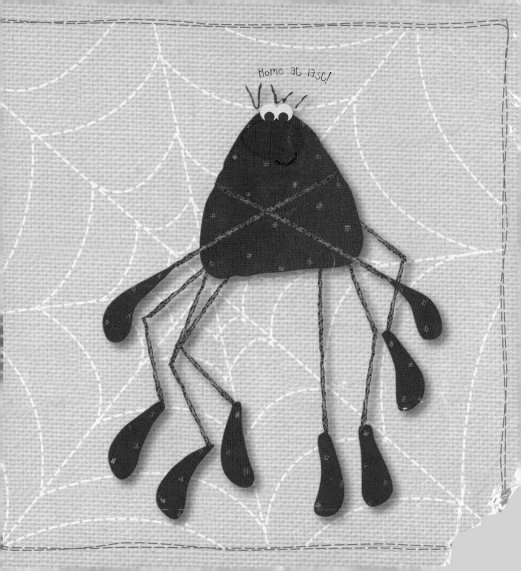

So **Incy Wincy Spider**
can climb the water spout.
And even if the **rain pours down**,
it can't wash **Incy** out.
For **Incy Wincy Spider**
has found **another** way,

and now it's "**easy-peasy**"